THE UNEXPURGATED ADVENTURES OF

SHERLOCK HOLMES

BOOK 10

THE MYSTERIOUS MARRIAGE OF THE GAY BACHELOR

by NP Sercombe

The un-edited manuscript originally entitled
The Adventure of the Noble Bachelor written by
Dr. John Watson and Sir Arthur Conan Doyle

Illustrations by Juliet Snape

Published by EVA BOOKS 2020 – c/o Harry King Films Limited
1&2 The Barn
West Stoke Road
Lavant
n/r Chichester
West Sussex PO18 9AA

A CIP catalogue record for this book is available from the British Library.

ISBN 978-1-9996961-9-1 (Hardback)

Book layout & cover design by Clare Brayshaw.

Cover illustration by Juliet Snape.

Set in Bruce Old Style.

Prepared and printed by: York Publishing Services Ltd
64 Hallfield Road, Layerthorpe, York YO31 7ZQ

Tel: 01904 431213

Website: www.yps-publishing.co.uk

THE UNEXPURGATED ADVENTURES OF

SHERLOCK HOLMES

Books in the Series:

Nicholas Sercombe is a writer and producer for film and television. He has been lucky enough to work in comedy for most of the Holocene period with some of the greatest performers and writers. He is most comfortable when reading Conan Doyle and even happier when re-writing these extraordinarily entertaining stories by Dr. John Watson.

Juliet Snape studied illustration at Cambridge School of Art and Central St. Martins. She has illustrated over 100 books and her work has been published around the world.

She is a fan of Sherlock Holmes – her father even lived in Baker Street – and, in the words of Conan Doyle, she is *"naturally gravitated to London, that great cesspool into which all the loungers and idlers of the Empire are irresistibly drained."* She lives in London and loves sketching, finding inspiration all around her. She has two children, both successful creatives.

Dedication

This book is dedicated to my friend, Puz, more formally known to the world as Derek Russell Stoneham, who died in the summer of this year. I have many fond memories of Puz. He was a great motivator who enjoyed connecting people with the sole purpose of making their lives more beautiful. If it hadn't been for him, these expanded versions of Holmes and Watson's adventures would not have been published. In fact, they would never have been written.

Nicholas Sercombe
9th October 2020

The Mysterious Marriage of the Gay Bachelor

(published in The Strand in April 1892 as
THE ADVENTURE OF THE NOBLE BACHELOR
by Dr. Watson and Arthur Conan Doyle)

The Lord St. Simon marriage, and its curious termination, have long since ceased to be a subject of interest in those exalted circles in which the unfortunate bridegroom moves. Fresh scandals have eclipsed it, and their more piquant details have drawn the gossips away from his lordship's embarrassing drama. As I have reason to believe, however, that the full facts have never been revealed to the general public and as my friend Sherlock Holmes had a considerable share in clearing the matter up, I feel that no memoir of him would be complete without some little sketch of this remarkable episode. His lordship may well be upset by the publication of the record – he may even set his lawyers upon me – but every word of this story is the truth, the whole truth and nothing but the truth so help me God. Who knows, he may even be impressed about my revelations of how cleverly the great detective acted behind the scenes on his behalf, especially with the blundering Inspector Lestrade of Scotland Yard, and the rising star of the criminal underworld, Professor Moriarty. These are facts that have never been revealed to the Lord St. Simon before.

It was the Spring of 1891. Sherlock Holmes came home to 221B Baker street from an afternoon stroll to find a letter waiting on the table for him. I had remained indoors all day, for the weather had taken a sudden turn to rain, with blustery seasonal winds, and the Jezail bullet which I had brought back in one of my limbs as a relic of my Afghan campaign, throbbed with dull persistency. With my body in one easy chair and my legs upon another, I had surrounded myself with a cloud of newspapers, until at last, saturated with news of the day, I tossed them aside and lay listless, my eye distracted by the huge crest and monogram printed on the envelope upon the table, and wondering lazily who my friend's noble correspondent should be.

'Here is a very fashionable epistle,' I remarked as he entered, saturated with the rain of the day. 'Your morning letters were, if I remember right, from a fishmonger and a tide-waiter, whatever that is.'

'Yes, my correspondence has certainly the charm of variety,' he answered, smiling, 'and a tide-waiter is a customs official who seeks out contraband. People like tide-waiters and fishmongers are usually more interesting than people who send this.' He picked up the monogrammed envelope and studied it. 'This looks like one of those unwelcome social summonses from some aristocrat or other who call upon a man like me either to be bored or to lie. Or it is similar to that demand you received from an aristocrat to explain why you rogered his daughter and put her into the family way!'

'Oh, Holmes, what are the chances of that happening ever again?'*

---

*   see *"A Misdemeanour in Middle Wallop* (written, unpublished (embargoed))

'Do you really wish me to give you some odds?'

We burst into laughter at the memory of the event, which had culminated in our hasty retreat – i.e. running away – from Beecher Manor in the middle of the night. Holmes and I streaked down the driveway in fear of our lives after Colonel Sir Hugh Bamberhoosie (Bt) caught yours truly giving his insatiable daughter, Morag, a right seeing-to and made skilful use of his grouse moor Purdeys.

'No, better not,' said he, still chuckling, 'I still have a pellet imbedded in my rear from the Colonel's lucky shot.'

'The cheeky shot!'

We laughed at the fond reminder of me operating on Holmes's *gluteus* under gaslight with scalpel and pincers to remove the rest of the Colonel's lead pellets. Later, it transpired, that I missed one.

'Talking of old war wounds, Holmes,' said I, rubbing my leg, 'the Jezail slug has been kicking up a hell of a fuss all afternoon. It must be the wet weather.'

'It is the very least you deserve, Watson. Maybe you should regard it as an occasional reminder not to interfere with our clients' daughters.'

Holmes broke the seal of the envelope and glanced over the contents. He raised his eyebrows, which was a tell-take sign of his intellectual interest.

'No social, then?'

'No, Watson. It is distinctly professional.'

'And from a noble client?'

'One of the highest in England.'

'My dear fellow, I congratulate you. Mind you, you said earlier that the working man generally throws up more interesting situations and dilemmas than the aristocracy and yet I find myself writing accounts of noble people more frequently than commoners. How can this be?'

'Shut up, Watson. I assure you, without affectation, that the status of my client here is a matter of less importance to me than the interest of his case. It is just possible, however, that that also may not be wanting in this new investigation. You have been reading the papers diligently of late, have you not?'

'Let's take a look at the evidence...' said I, sarcastically, whilst pointing to the huge bundle in the corner. 'I have had nothing else to do. Now that I have discarded my surgery and medical consultations I rely upon your clients to provide investigations for me to post up, and, just recently, those have been beset by problems.'

'Then this may be fortunate,' said he, waving the smart letter at me, 'I read nothing except the criminal news and the agony column. The latter is always instructive. But if you have followed recent events so closely you must have read about Lord St. Simon and his wedding?'

'Oh, yes, with the deepest interest.'

'That is well. The letter which I hold in my hands is from Lord St. Simon. I will read it to you, and in return you must turn over these papers and let me have whatever bears upon the matter. This is what he says:

'"My dear Mr. Sherlock Holmes, – Lord Backwater tells me that I may place implicit reliance upon your judgment and discretion. I have determined, therefore, to call upon you, and to consult you in reference to the very painful event which has occurred in connection with my wedding. Mr. Lestrade, of Scotland Yard, is acting already…"'

'The fool!'

'Oh, yes, I am afraid so, my dear Doctor,' said he. '"but he assures me that he sees no objection to your co-operation, and that he even thinks that it might be of some assistance."'

'The cheek of the man!'

'"I will call at four o'clock in the afternoon, and should you have any other engagement at that time, I hope you will postpone it, as this is a matter of paramount importance. – Yours faithfully, Robert St. Simon"'

'It is dated from Grosvenor Mansions, written with a quill pen, and the noble lord has had the misfortune to get a smear of ink upon the outer side of his right little finger,' remarked Holmes, as he folded up the epistle.

I glanced up to the Bahnhäusle wall clock, a recent gift to Sherlock Holmes from Herr Jurgen Hainhofer, the celebrated Füürtufel cheese merchant, in gratitude for delivering a daring poisoner to justice, and it was forty minutes past the hour of three. The new clock was a constant reminder to me of an adventure that I had been unable to write an account of, having been left behind in London by the great detective when he buggered off impromptu to Germany. During an evening last January, when Holmes and I had picked out a harlot each in Mother Kelly's and settled down in our chosen Chamber of Mercy when he was *interruptu* in his weekly allocation of *coitus* by an urgent telegram from Munich. The great detective was so excited by the commission he threw on his clothes and tore off to Victoria station, faster than Stephenson's Rocket. Hence, I bore no witness to the fascinating ingenuity and nuances used by Holmes to solve *The Case of the Furtwangen Jalapeño Poisoner*. Such was the narrative of the case and the image of such an exotic location that I am certain it would have been one of my finest instalments in *The Strand* magazine. A peculiar event was now lost forever.

'I say, Holmes, I really do hope that this St. Simon affair is not too dull. After all, I have missed out recently. I have an urgent need to post a colourful account with Newnes, what with me missing out as the reporter in Munich – your apology still pending – and then having an embargo placed upon the last account by Bamberhoosie's humourless solicitors.'

'How were we to know that Bamberhoosie and the judge went to Eton together?'

'The *same house* at Eton together, Holmes, and he is a godfather to Morag.'

'Yes, indeed. The interdiction will not be lifted until the baronet's death.'

'It is forty-five past three already. We have not much time before St. Simon arrives.'

'Then I have just time, with your assistance, to get clear upon the subject of this affair.'

'Just before we start, can I be clear on another subject? That is the matter of charging a fee to Lord St. Simon.' Holmes sighed and looked away, tapping his long white fingers on the nearby escritoire. 'Once again, we are skint and the rent is due on Wednesday. May I suggest we ask for cash upon engagement?'

'Skint? Such an army expression, Doctor, renders the Lord St. Simon no respect, such is his position as a senior aristocrat. We shall have none of the vain trivialities of money to taint our lordship's tale of woe. Turn over those papers, and arrange the extracts in their order of time, while I take a glance as to who our client is.' He picked a red-covered volume from a line of books of reference beside the mantelpiece. 'Here he is,' said he, sitting down and flattening it out upon his knee. '"Robert Walsingham de Vere St. Simon, second son of the Duke of Balmoral." Hmmm! What else? Ah! Arms...'

'Two, hopefully?'

'Shut up Watson! "*Coat of* Arms: azure, three caltrops in chief over a fess sable. Born in 1846." He is forty-one years of age, which is mature for a marriage. "Was Under-Secretary for the Colonies... in a recent Administration..." Blah, blah... "His father, the Duke, was at one time Secretary for Foreign Affairs..." They inherit the Plantagenet blood by direct descent, and Tudor on the distaff side. Ha! Well, there is nothing very instructive in all of this. I think I must turn to you, Watson, for something more insightful. Some juicy chit-chat. Some gossip!'

'I have very little difficulty in finding what I want,' said I, 'for the facts are quite recent, and the matter struck me as remarkable. I feared to refer them to you, however, as I knew that you had the cheese enquiry on hand, and that you disliked the intrusion of other matters.'

'Oh, and the Füürtufel was sublimely delicious. Please give me the results of your newspaper selections.'

'Sandown or Newmarket?'

Holmes gave me an anguished sigh. Clearly, he was not in a playful mood and certainly he preferred not to delve deeper into the horseracing that day. He resumed the tiresome tapping of his fingers.

'Sorry, Holmes... Here is the first notice. It is in the personal column of the Morning Post and dates, as you can see, some weeks back. "A marriage has been arranged," it says, "and will, if rumour is correct, very shortly take place, between Robert, Lord St. Simon, second son of the Duke of Balmoral, and Miss Hatty Trump, the only daughter of Aloysius Trump Esq,. of San Francisco, California, U.S.A." That is all.'

'Terse and to the point,' remarked Holmes, stretching his long legs towards the fire.

'There was a paragraph amplifying this one in one of the society papers of the same week. Ah, here it is. "There will be a call for protection in the marriage market, for the present free-trade principle appears to tell heavily against our home product. One by one the management of the noble houses of Great Britain is passing into the hands of our fair cousins from across the Atlantic. An important addition has been made during the last week to the list of prizes which have been borne away by these charming invaders. Lord St. Simon, who has shown himself for over twenty years proof against the little god's arrows, has now definitely announced his approaching marriage with Miss Hatty Trump, the fascinating daughter of a Californian millionaire. Miss Trump, whose graceful figure and striking face attracted much attention at the Westbury

House festivities, is an only child, and it is currently reported that her dowry will run to considerably over the six figures, with expectancies for the future. As it is an open secret that the Duke of Balmoral has been compelled to sell his pictures within the last few years, and as Lord St. Simon has no property of this own, save the small estate of Birchmoor, it is obvious that the Californian heiress is not the only gainer by an alliance which will enable her to make the easy and common transition from a Republican lady to a British title."'

'Anything else?' Asked Holmes, yawning.

'Yes, and I agree with you, thus far it bears the appearance of a tedious preface to your next investigation. But wait a moment, there is hope. There is plenty more here. There is another note in the *Morning Post* to say that the marriage would be an absolutely quiet one, that it would be at St. George's in Hanover Square, that only half a dozen intimate friends would be invited, and that the party would return to the furnished house at Lancaster Gate which has been taken by Mr. Aloysius Trump. Two days later – that is, on Wednesday last – there is a curt announcement that the wedding had taken place, and that the honeymoon would be passed at Lord Backwater's, near Petersfield. Those are all the notices which appeared before the disappearance of the bride.'

'Before the... did you say the disappearance of the bride?'

'Yes, Holmes. The vanishing of the lady.'

'When did she vanish then?'

'At the wedding breakfast.'

'Marvellous! This is more interesting than it promised to be; quite dramatic, in fact.'

'Yes, it struck me as being a little out of the common.' I rubbed my hands together in anticipation. 'This will make a fine account, Holmes!'

'I anticipate so, Doctor. Often the bride vanishes before the ceremony, and occasionally, during the honeymoon; but I cannot call to mind anything quite so prompt as this. Pray let me have the details.'

'I warn you that they are very incomplete.'

'Perhaps we shall make them less so. Read to me!'

'Such as they are, they are set forth in a single article of a morning newspaper of yesterday. It is headed: "Singular Occurrence at a Fashionable Wedding:" Are you sitting comfortably?'

'Look! I am standing. Get on with it, Watson.'

'Then I shall begin...' I flicked the broadsheet taut, like the crack of a recently tacked sail as its slack catches the breeze. 'Ahem!'

'Get on with it!'

'"The family of Robert, Lord St. Simon, has been thrown into the greatest consternation by the strange and painful episodes which have taken place in connection with his wedding. The ceremony, as shortly announced in the papers yesterday, occurred on the previous morning; but it is only now that it has been possible to confirm the strange rumours which have been so persistently floating about. In spite of the attempts of the friends to hush the matter up, so much public attention has now been drawn to it, that no good purpose can be served by affecting to disregard what is a common subject for conversation."

"The ceremony, which was performed at St. George's, Hanover Square, was a very quiet one, no one being present save the father of the bride, Mr. Aloysius Trump, The Duchess of Balmoral, Lord Backwater, Lord Eustace and Lady Clara St. Simon (the younger brother and sister of the bridegroom), and Lady Alicia Whittington. The whole party proceeded afterwards to the house of Mr. Aloysius Trump, at Lancaster Gate, where breakfast had been prepared. It appears that some little trouble had been caused by a woman, whose name has not been ascertained, who endeavoured to force her way into the house after the bridal party, alleging that she had some claim upon Lord St. Simon. It was only after a painful prolonged scene that she was ejected by the butler and the footman. The bride, who had fortunately entered the house before this unpleasant interruption, had sat down to breakfast with the rest, when she complained of a sudden indisposition, and retired to her room. Her prolonged absence having caused some comment, her father followed her; but learned from her maid that she had only come up to her chamber for an instant, caught up an ulster and bonnet, and hurried down the passage. One of the footmen declared that he had seen a lady leave the house apparelled; but had refused to credit that it was his mistress, believing her to be with the company. On ascertaining that his daughter had disappeared, Mr. Aloysius Trump, in conjunction with the bridegroom, instantly put themselves into communication with the police, and very energetic inquiries are being made, which will probably result in a speedy clearing up of this very singular business. Up to a late hour last night, however, nothing had transpired as to the whereabouts of the missing lady. There are rumours of foul play in the matter, and it is said that the police have arrested the woman who had caused the original disturbance, in the belief that, from jealousy or some other motive, she may have been concerned in the strange disappearance of the bride."'

'Is that it?'

'What do you mean, "is that it?" Of course, that is it.'

'No, really, Watson, *is* that *it*?'

Ah-ha! This old routine! 'All right Holmes...' I chuckled away at the fond memory of baiting Mr. Jabez Wilson.* 'That is enough of that!'

'Enough of what?'

'Enough of what you were referring to.'

'Enough of saying over and over "is that it?"'

'Oh, that. All right. Anything else?'

'That Miss Flora Miller , the lady who had caused the disturbance, has actually been arrested.'

'Ha! Only Inspector Lestrade could make such a bungle!'

'It appears she used to be a *danseuse* at the Allegro, and that she had known the bridegroom for some years.'

Holmes raised his eyebrows, as if he was familiar with this style of report – boy-meets-prostitute – and I heard him mumble something about "same old story..." before we heard the distant and familiar ring of the bell at the front door.

'It is approaching four o'clock, Watson. This is an exceedingly interesting case, and I wouldn't miss it for the world.'

---

* see *The Mysterious Case of Mr. Gingernuts*

'Likewise, Holmes. Not only will it make an exquisite story, he can afford to pay us as well.'

'Tsk! I perceive that must be our noble client arriving now, so let us find out what he has to say for himself.'

There was a knock on the door, and with Holmes's bidding of "Come!" Mrs. Hudson announced Lord St. Simon and ushered him into the room. Now, we were most fortunate to have sight of an Englishman who gave the appearance of being the very epitome of a gentleman. He strode slowly into the room, erect, turning his head slowly from left to right, placing his splendid walking stick with dignity aside each step and chose a spot to stop just under the new clock, firmly planting his silver-topped cane in front of him with both hands resting atop. He lifted his head up high to shine the light on his countenance so that he may scrutinise us and we may admire him. He was a handsome fellow with a pleasant, cultured face, high-nosed and pale, with something perhaps of a petulance about the mouth, and with the steady, well-opened eye of a man whose pleasant lot it had ever been to command and to be obeyed, a bearing that was suddenly shot to pieces by the toy doors clacking open on the face of the Bahnhäusle clock and a little blue bird launching herself out on a wire above his head.

"CUCKOO!"

The incongruity of this supreme aristocrat being ridiculed by Becky, the Bavarian blue tit, was pure comedy!

'How punctual you are, Lord St. Simon,' remarked the great detective, bowing from the waist. But suddenly Lord St. Simon's face turned red. He swung around to catch sight of "Becky" returning to her sanctity of the clock. She re-emerged almost instantly, only to be intercepted by the perfectly-timed silver knob of his lordship's cane, delivered at blisteringly high-speed. Becky was an instant hit, smashed to smithereens.

'Shot, sir!' Holmes ejaculated.

Lord St. Simon nodded to Sherlock Holmes. 'I have been on the grouse for the last two months. De Grey rates me as an equal. Well, almost…'

'A great compliment, sir. May I say, one can tell?'

Lord St. Simon nodded his appreciation. I was upset at the wanton destruction of this fine clock, which I was fond of, but was in no position to pass comment. But here was an irony to the situation I found myself in, that since I had abandoned my medical practice to become a roving reporter of my friend's investigations, I needed to engage any new client as much as Sherlock Holmes. Maybe our reasons for the engagements were different but Holmes and I were now entirely symbiotic – *ipso facto*, I was trapped in the orbit of this great man, for all of his faults. So, there were times, such as this one of aristocratic vandalism, when it was best to hold my tongue whilst my companion delivered diplomacy to secure new business. I watched him now – a class act – grinning serenely as he held his arm out in entreaty to the nobleman. After all, what loss was one tit in a Bavarian cuckoo clock?

'Pray, take the basket chair, sir. This is my friend and colleague, Doctor Watson. Draw up a little to the fire, and we shall talk this matter over.'

He sat, and Holmes drew up the Windsor rocking chair opposite. I took possession of the raspberry

Cuckoos were out of season but the Lord St. Simon still killed Becky with a single blow!

damask Savonarola a few feet further back into the room. Just as my posterior hit the cloth, Lord St. Simon gave me a withering look and turned to Holmes.

'What about this Doctor Watson fellow? Is he a gentleman, sir?'

'No, he is not.'

'I thought not. He has the grammar school look about him. I prefer to discuss this most painful matter to me upon a social level of my own, as you can most readily imagine, Mister Holmes, so you may dispose of him.'

'Sir, I would not dream of letting him go. I very much prefer having a witness, if only to check my own memory.'

'A type of secretary?'

'Yes.'

'Well, all right then, but he must not say a word in my presence.'

'Of course, sir,' oiled Holmes, and then turned to me with a wry smile on his features. This told me that secretly he was laughing his socks off and getting ready to play the fool. He stood up and glared at me.

'I say, you, Watson!' commanded he, flicking his long white fingers at me. 'Give his lordship some room to breathe. Move back. Make space!'

'Oh, yes, kind sirs!' said I, playing up to Lord Holmes's lead by pushing back on the chair's casters whilst summoning every nuance of sarcasm that I could find. 'And thank you *so much* for letting me stay!'

'Not a word!' barked Lord St. Simon straight at me. 'Now, Mister Holmes, let me begin...'

There was Sherlock Holmes, the offspring from a breeding pair of boffin scientists, now deemed to be a gentleman by this ludicrous nob sitting in front of me. Huh! Talk about condescending!

'I have been cut to the quick!' exclaimed the noble lord. 'I understand you have already managed several delicate cases of this sort, sir, though I presume that they were hardly from the same class of society.'

'No, I am descending.'

'I beg your pardon?!'

'My last client was a king.'

His last client was a king? The Füürtufel cheese merchant was the King of Switzerland? He never told me!

'Oh, really!' said Lord St. Simon. 'I had no idea. And which king?'

'The King of Bohemia.'*

'Why?' asked the noble lord, 'had he lost his wife?'

'You can understand,' said Holmes suavely, 'that I extend to the affairs of my other clients the same secrecy which I promise to you in yours.'

'Of course! Very right! Very right! I am sure I beg your pardon. As to my own case, I am ready to give you any information which may assist you in forming an opinion.'

'Thank you. I have already learned all that is in the public prints, nothing more. I presume that I may take it as correct – this article, for example, as to the disappearance of the bride.'

---

* see *A Balls-Up in Bohemia*

Lord St. Simon glanced over it. 'Yes, it is correct, as far as it goes.'

'But it needs a great deal of supplementing before anyone could offer an opinion,' added Holmes. 'I think that I may arrive at the facts most easily by directly questioning you.'

'Pray do so.'

'When did you first meet Miss Hatty Trump?'

'In San Francisco, a year ago.'

'You were travelling in the States?'

'Yes.'

'Did you become engaged then?'

'No.'

'But you were on a friendly footing?'

'I was amused by her society, and she could see that I was amused.'

'Her father is very rich?'

'He is said to be the richest man on the Pacific Slope.'

'And how did he make his money?'

'In mining. He had nothing a few years ago. Then he struck gold, invested it, and came up by leaps and bounds.'

'Now, what is your own impression as to the young lady's – your wife's character?'

The nobleman picked out his gold-rimmed glasses from his pocket and swung them around as he stared down into the fire. 'You see, Mister Holmes,' said he, 'my wife was twenty before her father became a rich man. During that time she ran free in a mining camp, and wandered through woods or mountains, so that her education has come from nature rather than from the schoolmaster. She is what we call in England a tomboy, with a strong nature – volcanic, I was about to say. She is swift in making up her mind, and fearless in carrying out her resolutions. On the other hand, I would not have given her the name which I have the honour to bear' (he gave a little stately cough) 'had I not thought her to be at bottom a noble woman. I believe she is capable of heroic self-sacrifice, and that anything dishonourable would be repugnant to her.'

Holmes and I glanced at one another. We agreed in silence, and by telepathy, that Miss Hatty was a right handful and an unlikely match. We had to doubt the judgment of this nobleman; he was, after all, getting himself involved with a tearaway who was completely uneducated in the ways of the English aristocracy.

'I can tell what you are thinking,' said he, in a manner of slight resignation, 'but a gentleman in my position must produce an heir. It is my duty, even if it is against my nature.' And he dipped his head in resignation. As a doctor, I could see how the penny dropped for this fellow and so despite his command that I should not interrupt the interview, it became my duty to over-ride that instruction.

'Ah, I see...' said I. 'That fact that Miss Hatty is a tomboy – therefore, more of a boy than a girl, both in action and appearance – even though, medically speaking, and I am a doctor, she is definitely a girl, through and through, is more attractive – shall we say alluring? – to your lordship than marrying a more *feminine* girl. Am I correct?'

'WILL YOU KEEP QUIET!' barked Lord St. Simon. 'It is nothing to do with the sort! Not shirt lifting nor fudging, sir!' Then, he calmed a little... 'I prefer to lead the life of a gay bachelor, the cornucopia of beautiful women being at my behest due to my fortunate birth of position and title, and it being against my nature to be monogamous! Yes, one could opine that her masculine features were not essential to make the marriage successful but her marriage contract is, and my family and I are more interested in her child-bearing age and physique. She would bring healthy heirs to the dukedom.'

The noble peer allowed Holmes and I a moment of consideration about the attraction of her father's enormous wealth and how bountiful the aforementioned marriage contract must be.

'Have you a photograph?' asked Holmes, eventually.

'I brought this with me.' He opened a locket and showed us the full face of a very lovely woman. It was an ivory miniature and I suspect the artist had been paid handsomely to bring out the full effect of the lustrous black wavy hair and the large eyes whist reducing the prominence of the square chin and wide mouth. Holmes and I gazed long and earnestly at it. Now I could understand why Lord St. Simon's judgment had been deviated; when I added what I presumed to be an enormous dowry to the mixture, she was a hot recipe, even if she did look a little like my nephew. Holmes closed the locket and handed it back to Lord St. Simon.

'The young lady came to London. Then, you renewed your acquaintance?'

'Yes, her father brought her over for this last London season and took a house in Sussex Gardens. I met her several times, became engaged to her, and have now married her.'

'She brought, I understand, a considerable dowry.'

'It is absolutely gigantic. As far as Mr. Trump is concerned, a marriage contract with such a noble family as mine is a step up in life; and, to have me, the most noble and eligible of all the bachelors in England, is a dream come true. Therefore, my dear sir, he must pay.'

'And this dowry, of course,' said Holmes, 'remains with you, since the marriage is a *fait accompli*?'

'I really have made no enquiries upon the subject.'

'Very naturally not. Did you see Miss Trump on the day before the wedding?'

'Yes.'

'Was she in good spirits?'

'Never better. She kept talking of what we should do in our future lives.'

'Indeed. That is very interesting. And on the morning of the wedding?'

'She was as bright as possible – at least, until after the ceremony.'

'And did you observe any change in her then?'

'Well, to tell the truth, I saw then the first signs that I had ever seen that her temper was just a little sharp. The incident, however, was too trivial to relate, and can have no possible bearing upon the case.'

'Pray, let us have it, for all that.'

'Oh, it is childish. She dropped her bouquet as we went towards the vestry. She was passing the front pew at the time, and it fell over into the pew. There was a moment's delay, but the gentleman in the pew handed it up to her again, and it did appear to be the worse for the fall. Yet, when I spoke to her of the matter, she answered me abruptly; and in the carriage, on our way home, she seemed absurdly agitated over this trifling cause.'

'Indeed. You say that there was a gentleman in the pew. Some of the general public were present then?'

'Unfortunately, a church is a public building, Mister Holmes. One cannot exclude the riff-raff or withhold access to the great unwashed.'

'This gentleman was not one of your wife's friends?'

'Certainly not, sir! I call him a gentleman only by courtesy.'

'What did he look like?'

'Tall, about your height. Dark. Handsome. A tall, youthful face, notable because of its long, tonsured moustaches. He was very well-dressed.'

'Not like Doctor Watson here?'

'Yes, absolutely!''

I forced a smile, rather like a puppy-dog glove puppet.

'But, Mister Holmes, he had an air about him that was very dangerous. No man would challenge that fellow to a duel.'

'Did he have dark green eyes?'

'Dammit, Mister Holmes! I am not in the habit of gazing into a gentlemen's eyes. Are we not wandering from the point?'

'My apologies, your lordship, but I require more details. I crave your indulgence.'

Unluckily for Holmes, Lord St Simon didn't like to gaze into men's eyes …

'Details? If you require more details from me there will be no more quips, sir!'

'I agree. Shut up, Watson!'

'Me?'

'Yes, you!' exclaimed the Lord St. Simon as he jabbed his forefinger at me 'Do not speak another word in my presence!'

He turned back to Holmes, who flicked me a look that requested my cooperation to indulge this frightful person's manners. My eyes, I obliged him! Holmes leaned forward to bring his line of inquiry back on track.

'Lady St. Simon, then,' said he, 'returned from the wedding in a less cheerful frame of mind than she had gone to it. What did she do on re-entering her father's house?'

'I saw her in conversation with her maid.'

'And who is her maid?'

'Alice is her name. She is an American and came from California with her.'

'A confidential servant?'

'A little too much so. It seemed to me that her mistress allowed her to take great liberties. Still, of course, in America they look upon these things in a different way.'

'How long did she speak to this Alice?'

'Oh, a few minutes. I had something else to think of.'

'You did not overhear what they said?'

'Lady St. Simon said something about "jumping a claim." She was accustomed to use slang of the kind. I have no idea what she meant.'

'American slang is very expressive sometimes. And what did your wife do when she had finished speaking to her maid?'

'She walked into the breakfast room.'

'On your arm?'

'No, alone. She was very independent in little matters like that. Then, after we had sat down for ten minutes or so, she rose hurriedly, muttered some words of apology, and the left the room. She never came back.'

'But this maid, Alice, as I understand, deposes that she went to her room, covered her bride's dress with a long ulster, put on a bonnet, and went out.'

'Quite so. and was afterwards seen walking into Hyde Park in company with Flora Millar, a woman who is now in custody, and who had already made a disturbance at Mr. Trump's house that morning.'

'Ah, yes. I should like to take a few particulars as to this young lady, and your relations with her.'

'Lord St. Simon shrugged his shoulders and raised his eyebrows. 'We have been on a friendly footing for many years – I may say on a *very* friendly footing. She used to be at the Allegro.'

Ah! She was the *danseuse* referred to in the papers. It was on her behalf that Cupid had planted an arrow squarely on his dickiedoodah.

'I have not treated her ungenerously, and she has no just cause of complaint against me, but you know what women are, Mister Holmes. Flora was a dear little thing but exceedingly hot-headed, and devotedly attached to me. She wrote me dreadful letters when she heard that I was to be married, and to tell the truth the reason why I had the marriage celebrated so quietly was that I feared lest there might be a scandal in the church. She came to Mr. Trump's door just after we returned, and she endeavoured to push her way in, uttering very abusive expressions towards my wife, and even threatening her, but I had foreseen the possibility of something of the sort, and I had given instructions to the servants, who soon pushed her out again. She was quiet when she saw that there was no good in making a row.'

'Did you wife hear all this?'

'No, thank goodness, she did not.'

'And she was seen walking with this very woman afterwards?'

'Yes. That is what Mister Lestrade, of Scotland yard, looks upon as so serious. It is thought that Flora decoyed my wife out.'

'Well, it is a possible supposition. It is terribly bad form to have one's wife consorting with one's mistress, even a professional tart like yours. Anybody would think that we were French.'

'Ha, Mister Holmes! You have made me smile for the first time since the start of this terrible affair. You think so too?'

'I did not say a probable one. But you do not yourself look upon this as likely?'

'I do not think Flora would hurt a fly.'

'Still, jealousy is a strange transformer of character. Pray what is your own theory as to what took place?'

'Well, really, I came to seek a theory, not to propound one. I have given you all the facts. Since you ask me, however, I may say that it has occurred to me as possible that the excitement of this affair, the consciousness that she had made so immense a social stride marrying me, the noblest noble in the land, had the effect of causing some little nervous disturbance in my wife.'

Holmes nodded. I nodded, sarcastically, which made Holmes bulge his eyes at me. Well, really, the man's humility knew no bounds!

'In short,' enquired Holmes, trying to distract Lord St. Simon away from looking in my direction, 'that she had become suddenly deranged?'

Lord St. Simon stood up, stretched to full his height, and stood erect, with his back turned towards me. He presented himself to Sherlock Holmes from nose to floor with a graceful, sweeping movement of his right arm. 'Just look at me, Mister Holmes. Which woman would turn their back on this, the finest example of an English aristocrat anywhere in the world, unless she was deranged? There cannot be any other explanation.'

How ridiculous was his arrogance? I started to giggle, but I dared not make the slightest noise in fear of causing offence. I lowered my head, hiding my face, but then I caught my companion winking at me. That did it! I started to laugh, and laugh, and laugh. Medically speaking, I fell into a type of pseudobulbar effect – the involuntary act in the form of an acute convulsion — or, corpsing, as they say in the theatre. I could not stop!

'Well, certainly that is a conceivable hypothesis, your lordship!' said Holmes as drily as a country pastor, then winking at me again, his view of me still obscured by the most noble backside in the land. This was too much! I was trapped, inescapably, in the spasms. I was forced to jump up out of the Savonarola and make a dash for the door, where I stopped in the vestibule to recover my wits. At the same moment, Lord St. Simon dropped himself back into his chair, and I was within his peripheral vision,

'What is the matter with your secretary?'

'A pollen allergy, Lord St. Simon. It makes his eyes water.'

'I pity the working classes! They seem to have all sorts of pathetic ailments.'

'So true. Watson catches anything. Now, your lordship, I think that I have nearly all my data. May I ask whether you were seated at the breakfast table, so that you could see out of the window?'

'We could see the other side of the road, and the Park.'

'Quite so. Then I do not think that I need to detain you any longer. I shall communicate with you.'

'Should you be fortunate enough to solve this problem,' said our new client, rising from his seat.

'I have solved it.'

'Eh? What was that?'

'I say, I have solved it.'

'Where, then is my wife?'

'That is in the detail which I shall speedily supply.'

Having calmed my spasms and dried my eyes I walked back into the room, just in time to catch Lord St. Simon shaking his noble head.

'I am afraid that it will take wiser heads than yours or mine.' he remarked, and bowing in a stately, old-fashioned manner, he moved to depart. I saw him out and closed the door behind him.

'Ah, do you know, Watson, that it is very good of Lord St. Simon to honour my head by putting it on a level with his own,' said Sherlock Holmes, laughing.

'Holmes – the man is a complete and utter nob!'

'Yes, but he cannot help himself from being so, such is his upbringing. I think that I shall have a whisky and soda and a cigar after all this cross-questioning. I had formed my conclusions as to the case before our client came into the room.' He added a seraphic grin.

'My dear Holmes!' said I, as I poured two tumblers of Loch Sturgeon ten-year-old from the sideboard decanter.

'I have notes of several similar cases, though none, as I remarked before, which were quite so prompt. My whole examination served to turn my conjecture into a certainty. Circumstantial evidence is occasionally very convincing, as when you find a trout in the milk, to quote Thoreau's example.'

What on Earth was he on about?

'But Holmes, I have never heard of this chap, Thoreau, or his trout, and I have heard all that you have heard and cannot begin to deduce an answer.'

'You have heard all that you have heard, Watson, without, however, the knowledge of pre-existing cases, which serves me so well. There was a parallel instance in Aberdeen some years back, and something on very much the same lines as Munich the year after the Franco-Prussian War. The antagonism in Lord St. Simon's instance, Watson, is our old friend: money. The over-riding clue to solving this minor mystery lies in the identity of the man in the church. Does that not give you the answer you seek, Doctor?'

No, it darned well did not! I shook my head in ignorance whilst Homes grinned from ear to ear in derisory amusement. But before I could extract more clues from the ebullient detective there was a knock at the door.

'But hallo, here is Lestrade! Good afternoon, Lestrade! You will find an extra tumbler upon the sideboard, and there are cigars in the box.'

Inspector Lestrade! Now, here was a contest for Sherlock Holmes that far exceeded the calibre of the noble client, both men in search of a solution to the same problem but approaching it from distinctly different angles. I could look forward to a sparring bout worthy of a ringside seat, especially with Sherlock Holmes in such high spritis. I rubbed my hands together in anticipation!

The official detective was attired in a pea-jacket and cravat, which gave him a decidedly nautical appearance, and he carried a black canvas bag in his hand. With a short greeting he seated himself and lit the cigar which had been offered to him. With all three of us puffing on the fine Havana's the room was thick with sweet smelling smoke; it became quite a fug.

'What's up, then?' asked Holmes, with a twinkle in his eye. 'You look dissatisfied.'

'And I feel dissatisfied. It is this infernal St. Simon marriage case. I can make neither head nor tail of this business.'

'Really? You surprise me.'

'Who ever heard of such a mixed affair! Every clue seems to slip through my fingers. I have been at work upon it all day.'

*Inspector Lestrade, puffed too hard on a heavy-duty
Havana and turned as green as a cabbage!*

'And very wet it seems to have made you,' said Holmes, laying his hand upon the arm of the pea-jacket.

'Yes, I have been dragging the Serpentine.'

'In Heaven's name, what for?'

'In search of the body of Lady St. Simon.'

Sherlock Holes leaned back in his chair and laughed heartily.

'Have you dragged the basin of the Trafalgar Square fountain?' he asked.

'Why? What do you mean?'

'Because you have just as good a chance of finding this lady in the one as in the other.'

Lestrade shot an angry glance at my companion. 'I suppose you know all about it,' he snarled.

'Well, I have only just heard the facts, but my mind is made up.'

'Oh, indeed?! Then you think the Serpentine plays no part in this matter?'

'I think it very unlikely.'

'Then perhaps you will kindly explain how it is that we found this in it?' He opened his bag as he spoke and tumbled on to the floor a wedding dress of watered silk, a pair of white satin shoes, and a bride's wreath and veil, all discoloured and soaked in water. 'There!' said he, putting a new wedding-ring upon the top of the pile. 'There is a little nut for you to crack, Master Holmes!'

'Oh, indeed,' said my friend, blowing blue rings of cigar smoke up towards the ceiling. He did this by forcing his cheek muscles inwards to form a circular shape with his mouth and then pushing the inhaled smoke out in short, sharp bursts. He looked just like the trout that he referred to just now!

'So, Lestrade, you dragged them from the Serpentine?'

'No, they were found floating near the margin by a park-keeper. They were identified as her clothes, and it seemed to me that if they were there the body would not be far off.'

'By the same brilliant reasoning, every man's body is to be found in the neighbourhood of his wardrobe. And pray what did you hope to arrive at through this?'

'At some evidence implicating Flora Millar in the disappearance.'

'I am afraid you will find it difficult.'

'Are you indeed, now?' cried Lestrade, with some bitterness and a lot more angst topped off with a sprinkling of elation. 'I am afraid, Holmes, that you ae not very practical with your deductions and your inferences. You have made two blunders in as many minutes. The dress does implicate Miss Flora Millar.'

'Really! And how?'

'In the dress is a pocket. In the pocket is a card-case. In the card-case is a note. And here is the very same note.' He slapped it down upon the table in front of him. 'Listen to this. "You will see me when all is ready. Come at once. F.H.M." Now my theory all along has been that Lady St. Simon was decoyed away by Flora Millar, and that she, with confederates no doubt, was responsible for her disappearance. Here, signed with her initials, is the very note which was no doubt quietly slipped into her hand at the door, and which lured her within their reach.'

'Very good, Lestrade,' said Holmes, laughing. 'You really are very fine indeed. Let me see it.' He took up the paper is a listless way, but his attention instantly became riveted, and he gave a little cry of satisfaction. 'This is indeed important!' he said.

'Ha, you find it so!'

'Extremely so. I congratulate you warmly.'

Lestrade rose in triumph, blowing a full lungful of smoke before him. 'Mister Holmes!' he shrieked, 'you are looking on the wrong side!'

'On the contrary, this is the right side.'

'The right side? You are mad! Here is the note written in pencil over here.' Lestrade collapsed back into his chair.

'And over here is what appears to be a fragment of a hotel bill, which interests me deeply.'

'There's nothing in it. I looked at it before.,' said Lestrade. '"October 4th, rooms 8s., breakfast 2s.6d., cocktail 1s., lunch 2s.6d., glass sherry 8d." I see nothing in that.'

''Very likely not. It is most important all the same. As to the note, it is important also, or at least the initials are, so, I congratulate you again.'

'I have wasted enough time,' muttered Lestrade, petulantly, rising up from his chair again. 'I believe in hard work, and not in sitting by the fire spinning fine theories. Good day, Mister Holmes! We shall see which gets to the bottom of the matter first.' He chucked the remain of his cigar into the fire, gathered up his garments, thrust them into the bag, and made for the door.

'Just one moment, Inspector!' piped Holmes, languishing lower into his seat and forcing his most seraphic of smiles. 'Here's a hint to you, and it is the true solution of the matter...'

Sherlock Holmes stood up, for full dramatic effect, and blew a cloud of smoke in the direction of Inspector Lestrade. He just couldn't let the policeman off the hook, could he?

'Lady St. Simon is a myth. There is not, and there never has been, any such person.'

Lestrade gaped at his rival and shook his head from side to side. Then he turned to me, tapped his forehead three times, shook his head solemnly, and hurried away.

He had hardly shut the door behind him when Holmes rose and put on his overcoat.

'There is something in what the inspector says about outdoor work,' he remarked, 'so I think, Watson, that we must leave the comfort of our apartment and venture out.'

'At least I know which hat you will be selecting.'

'Indeed so, Watson!' said Holmes, positioning the deerstalker upon his head. 'You are enhancing the powers of deduction more commonly as each day passes!'

* * *

Mr. Sherlock Holmes pulled the *Lestrade* down upon his brow and gave the lions' head knocker a firm tap on the front door of Chichester House, maybe the grandest residence that I could see in the neighbourhood of Sussex Gardens. You may remember, dear adventure enthusiast, that the great detective would wear his deerstalker only upon engagements where Inspector Lestrade was on the case, thus, as previously demonstrated, with one sharp pull of the drawstring he could release the ear flaps, pull them tight under his chin and protect his ears from the policeman's inane theories and deductions, or at least reduce them to muffled babblings.* Hence, its soubriquet.

The door was opened by a tall, burly butler who admitted us upon a matter-of-fact explanation of our presence. One could tell that he was a rental for no dedicated, loyal family servant of such high rank would allow access to his master on such a flimsy excuse.

Soon we were seated in the oak-panelled drawing room on one of the Chesterfields by the fireplace. In front of us was a tray of tea sitting on a poof. The Californian man who was hiring all of this made his entrance by entering the room with purpose; he had a strange way of walking, as if he had just jumped off a horse and was about to kick the saloon doors into next week. He was a man on a mission. He was about five eight, but he appeared to be making an attempt to be taller, his back straight as a ramrod. The look on his face was one of grim determination that told me he was meeting us only out of necessity. He stopped in front of us, his blue eyes staring out from under a mop of flaxen hair, and his right arm flipped up like a mechanical semaphore. With a curt "Hiya. I'm Trump," Holmes and I took turns to shake his hand and made our introductions. He seemed to blanche at the idea of meeting a private detective but waved us to be seated again and took his place on a matching Chesterfield opposite. The rental poured the tea whilst Mr. Trump

---

*   see *My First Proper Rural Murder*

sat back in his sofa and delivered his thoughts to us, not only in English but also in his own, local dialect.

'The cops have been runnin' in and outta this place like there's an election on,' expounded he, arms waving about the place. 'You say you're a private detective? And you, his secretary? Well now, Mister Holmes, those boys are from Scotland Yard. Well, ain't that where the real professionals hang out? Yes, sir! It is. And today, Mister Holmes, they brought me some hardcore evidence. Inspector Lestrade found my little Hatty's wedding dress, her shoes and her bridal bouquet in the lake. So, Mister Holmes, I ask you: what can you possibly bring to me that knocks that sorta bona fides crap outta the park? Are you wasting my time?'

'Maybe your daughter should be answering those questions,' said Holmes, placing his cup ever-so-delicately onto its saucer. Then, no doubt because of the mention of Lestrade by name, he fingered his deerstalker, fiddling with the cords that bound the flaps together.

Mr. Aloysius Trump leaped to his feet, thrust his right arm at the great detective. 'Don't you realise my daughter is dead? She is lost! She is drowned!'

'No she is not. I can assure you of that.'

Holmes's words hit Trump straight in the face, as if he had been slapped with a wet haddock. I have to tell you, dear adventure enthusiast, I wasn't warming to the brash Mr. Trump. The thought crossed my mind about where I may lay my hands upon a haddock...

'Don't play with me, sir!' cried he. 'Inspector Lestrade told me to dissipate *any* hope of his finding her alive.'

'She is alive and well.'

'You bring no evidence with you, not even a dimes-worth! Who do you think you are, Mister Holmes? Some sorta soothsayer?'

'No, Mister Trump, I read prolifically, but not tea leaves.' He waved his long white fingers in the direction of the tea pot on the poof. 'I read accounts about other misfortunate events such as this. I study facts. I make deductions.'

'That's all too damned fancy for me! I have no reason to believe that you are any better than Lestrade of Scotland `Yard. Why, he's the real thing, Mister Holmes. What do you know that he does not?'

Uh-oh! This was usually when storm clouds darkened Holmes's face as he prepared to put a misinformed man like Trump to the sword. But it was not to be on this occasion. Instead, Sherlock Holmes simply chuckled to himself.

'That is a question answered easily, Mister Trump. Not long after the public announcement of the engagement of your daughter to Lord St. Simon, you were visited by a tall, dark stranger. This man changed your daughter's life forever.'

Our host, a man who had been wallowing in his opinionated confidence, deteriorated rapidly. His head jolted upwards, as if he had been shot, and his jaw dropped like an attic door. Whilst he was in this slightly stupefied vacuum I decided to step in for my good friend and put the boot in.

'I'll wager that Inspector Lestrade never made mention of such a man,' said I, not being able to resist popping him a toothy grin.

Trump's eyes bulged wide. He thrust his arm forward at us once again. 'You are correct, sir! But if you are so clever, Mister Holmes, tell me what was the stranger's business?'

'The man demanded money from you. You refused to give it to him.'

'HOW DO YOU KNOW THAT?' shouted Mr. Aloysius Trump, throwing up his arms in despair and then dropping his whole body dramatically onto the Chesterfield. It was a very well sprung sofa, so Holmes and I watched him right himself from the bounce, then over-compensate, then right himself again and finally, when he had regained control, bury his face into his hands. He let out a long moan of anguish and kept repeating: 'Just *how* do you know? How? Just *how*!'

Sherlock Holmes waited. He dipped his head slightly and closed his eyes until Mr. Trump had settled himself. Holmes met his level, poker-faced, and flashed open his peepers.

'Because you have just told me,' he whispered slowly.

Mr. Trump jumped up from his Chesterfield. 'You are wizard, sir!'

Sherlock Holmes nodded. I raised my brows to him and looked over to Mr. Trump, who was now very excited.

'It is not the first time that Mister Holmes has been called a wizard,' said I. 'And you will find that Inspector Lestrade of Scotland Yard will not be in a position to have anybody make the same claim on his behalf.'

Mr. Trump ran around the poof and threw open his arms to us in entreaty.

'I agree with you, Doctor Watson! I am sorry to have doubted you, Mister Holmes. Where is she? Where is my dear little Hatty?'

Hmmm! I doubted whether the tomboy as described to us earlier was quite like that...

'I shall reunite you with her this evening,' said Holmes, standing up. 'Now, you will please allow me to make use of your butler to run an errand to that end?'

'If it means I get to see my Hatty you may take him home with you, if you please, Mister Holmes!' cried Aloysius Trump triumphantly.

'Good. Then at seven o'clock you will join us for supper at 221B Baker Street. Come, Watson – we must be on our way.'

* * *

We left Chichester House and dropped down the steps into Sussex Gardens. Whilst I hailed the nearest Hansom, Holmes dropped a note into the rental's hand and added a few verbal orders. Once we had caught the eye of a cab driver, I took the opportunity to ask him about it.

'It is an instruction, Watson,' said he, very matter-of-fact, 'to a caterer in St. James. We shall be hosting a supper party with a difference at 221B Baker Street this evening.'

'Should we not alert Mrs. Hudson?'

'After what we found out about her during Ascot week, Watson? That will not be necessary. She is hardly a woman of a frail character.'*

---

* see *The Adventure of the Engineer's Tongue*

The cab drew to a halt beside me.

'Driver!' said I. 'To 221B Baker Street.'

'No, driver,' said Holmes. 'Take us to St. Paul's church in Covent Garden.'

We sat quietly in the cab as it rattled through west London, past the Marble Arch, along Oxford Street – the bum crack of London – over Regent Street and down the hill into Covent Garden. It was only when we were winding our way down the rather narrow Sheraton Street, towards the church, that I passed a casual remark to the great detective about Mr. Trump and his foolish fantasy about Scotland Yard being the only professional detectives, and how we had soon shown him how wrong he could be.

'Believe me, Watson, that man has gone through a terrible personal torment. He was given the opportunity to give his daughter a second chance in her life and, up until we made our little visit, he thought that his actions had been the cause of her death. You remember how Lord St. Simon described Miss Hatty?'

'I do, Holmes. As a tomboy.'

'And, during her most formative years, that tomboy that had grown into Miss Hatty as a result of her father's absenteeism whilst he made his fortune, causing them both more relationship anxiety than a father and his pubescent daughter might normally have. But then there is a redemption, and that redemption is delivered in spades, in the shape and form of Lord St. Simon, England's most noble of bachelors. But just as the doting father gives his blessing to this new chapter in her life, he is thrown into a terrible dilemma.'

'My word, Holmes, what sort of dilemma?'

'One which only gains my full admiration for Mister Aloysius Trump.'

'Now, Holmes. On the one hand you seem to blame Mister Trump for this sordid business but then on the other you sing his praises. I am confused.'

'Not for much longer, Watson. Sharpen your pencil! Here we are at St. Paul's. Pay the driver, man, and let us make our way to the vestry.'

The front of the church faces the piazza and is rather grand, what with its columns and tilt to Roman architecture, a comment I made as we disembarked onto the steps, only to be met with an exhaustingly disdainful retort of: "Etruscan, Watson, Etruscan..." A brisk walk around the side to the rear of the building found us looking at two oak doors set into a large wooden panel with old iron strap hinges and a small, railed window. Holmes pushed the door open and we entered the building. Here was the strange thing – one would have thought that we had entered by the back door, so to speak because this was a church, but in fact we had gone in by the front because the altar and the chancel were set out before us at the far end of the nave. It was a church that seemed to be laid out the wrong away around but, of course, it was not because we were facing east. Are you confused, dear adventure enthusiast? Take courage from the fact that you are not as befuddled as the architect, Mr. Inigo Jones, who, to make such a balls-up, must have been on stronger stuff than Sherlock Holmes.

As we walked down the nave towards the altar, my curiosity overcame me. 'I say, Holmes, perhaps you could enlighten this observer and reporter of the reason for us to be here?'

'To make use of the Reverend Burton's communication services.'

I looked up at the ceiling and surveyed the space all around us; north, south, east and west.

'Would there *really* and *truly* be a telephone here, in a church?'

'There's no need for sarcasm, Watson. Just you wait and see.'

'But the Reverend Burton? My word, Holmes, that name rings a bell...' Suddenly I was in a quandary as to where I had heard the name before. It was not for long. Holmes, seeing my confusion, whispered "Nanny Moriarty" into my ear. Then it all came flooding back to me, a couple of years ago, when Holmes and I sat by Nanny Moriarty's death-bed, pumping her full of amphetamines (and anything else we could find in my medical bag), to keep her alive long enough to unload her memories and hand out advice to Sherlock Holmes.* The Reverend Burton was a name within that revelation. Now, for the life of me, I could not remember why.

We turned right at the altar and knocked on the door of the vestry. It was opened by one of the most impressive men I had ever first clapped eyes upon. There he was, staring back at me with stone-cold eyes, six foot four if an inch, with leading-man looks and a visage that stood no nonsense – even at fifty years there were no laughter lines on this man's face. He studied us carefully – first Sherlock Holmes and then me – which set off that inner twinge that one experiences when suddenly scared, the one where a bolt of electricity hits

---

* see *The Oranges of Death!*

one's wedding tackle, belts through the waste disposal department, bounces off the emergency exit and shoots up the rear drainpipe to tell you that something is terribly wrong. This man's very appearance sparked such electricity. Anyway, since neither man wished to speak, I stepped in to breach the gap.

'The Reverend Burton?' queried I, querulously.

'This is he, I can assure you,' said Holmes, never taking his eyes off Burton.

'I am the Reverend Burton. I can make a heaven of hell, or a hell of a heaven, Doctor Watson,' said he in a voice of mellifluous molten lava tinged with a Swansea lilt. How did he know my name?! He turned to face my companion. 'What is your pleasure, Mister Sherlock Holmes? Whilst God was still breathing air into your lungs I knew that it was only a matter of time before you would arrive upon this threshold. And here you are, like Odysseus washed up on Scherie, naked and exhausted, in great anticipation of what he is about to discover.'

Even from the perspective of my rather mediocre education, this language seemed to be a tad over-the-top. I glanced at the great detective, whose classical knowledge was second to many but still outstanding, and, sure enough, his face was impervious to such gobbledegook.

'Why don't you show us what I came here for, Reverend?' said Holmes.

'I am ready for you, my Lord' said he, in an unfathomly deep timbre 'Follow me along the path of your destiny but do not stray along the route and be mindful to keep your peace, for the Rector Cumberlege is preparing for Evensong.'

This was all too much! We walked down a stone passage and passed a few rooms, one of which was occupied and had the door ajar. I peeked a look inside and there was another fellow with leading-man looks – the Rector Cumber-something? Cumberbatch? Cumberdash? Anyway, there he was, seated in his armchair, and on first glance I thought he was a doppelgänger for Sherlock Holmes. Fanciful! Anyway, he was seated in the epitome of an ecclesiastical setting, reading the Good Book, a schooner of sherry to hand and puffing on a church warden. He felt my gaze upon him and flicked his eyes up. My goodness, he was young, and here was another face draped by a mop of curly hair. And what an overwhelming presence! He started to read to me, his voice and being drawing me in like a tugboat:

"How can I live without thee, how forgoes
Thy sweet Converse and Love so dearly joyn'd,
To live again in these wilde Woods forlorn?
Should God create another Eve, and I
Another Rib afford, yet loss of thee
Would never from my heart; no, I feel
The link of Nature draw me: Flesh of Flesh,
Bone of my Bone thou art, and from thy State
Mine never shall be parted, bliss or woe"

'That is your composition for Evensong, Rector?' enquired I, politely.

'No! It is Milton, you grammar school ignoramus!'

'Do not dally, Doctor,' drawled the Welsh brogue off some way down the passage. 'Come hither!'

With a "thank you very much, Rector," I continued my journey down the passage. As we climbed a narrow and winding stone staircase I couldn't help wondering how the Rector knew that I had attended grammar school. Then, I pondered the question: why there was such a cluster of dramatic vicars in St. Paul's?

We emerged upon the roof of the church. There was an odd-shaped shed to our right that we could reach easily enough by walking down a lead-lined gully. The Reverend Burton clicked the Yorkshire latch and bade us go inside. We walked into a space that was not dissimilar to a wooden airing cupboard, the difference being the air which filled our nostrils; instead of soap and fresh linen we had dank animal odours – the heady aroma of barley, and the whiff of animal excrement, but the type of dung that does not offend the olfactory so much as to seek cover or flight. I looked around us, at all the bar-fronted cages stacked up on layers of shelving, and I realised that we had arrived in a wonderland of... pigeons! Yes, this was the Reverend Burton's communication facility. Not a telephone, but carrier pigeons! There were all sorts. Many different shapes, colours and sizes. There are, apparently, well over one thousand species of pigeon.

'Here we have a Norwich Cropper,' reported our host, in a voice that was pouring treacle. 'Next there is a German Trumpeter. Over there, the Black Dragoons. And the favourite of our dear monarch, Queen Victoria, the Red Barb. There are Red Jacobins, Danish Tumblers and those two beauties over there are my latest edition.' The Reverend Burton pointed to a new cage above a window.

'They, Watson, are a pair of Hungarian Fairy Swallows. A rarity in England.'

'Ahhhh....' drawled Burton appreciatively. 'Now I can see why the Professor finds you such a formidable talent, Mister Holmes.'

How?! How on Earth could Sherlock Holmes have such intimate knowledge of pigeons? But he would know all about them, wouldn't he?

The Reverend pointed to a very large grey bird, sitting solitary in a coup. 'You don't see many of those around either, Mister Holmes.'

'You have a Giant Runt, Reverend.'

'There is really no need, Holmes!' I exclaimed.

'Shut up Watson! If at some point in your life you had taken the trouble to read *Fulton's Book of Fancy Pigeons* you would not have mistaken the Giant Runt for something more delicate. And with less plumage.'

'There are a few other odds and bods around the place; some racers, some rollers but mostly carriers. Now, Mister Holmes, it is one of these that you seek to hire from me today to reach my employer. Go ahead; see if you can pick the right one. If you succeed the Professor will be reading your message within the hour. If you fail, the good doctor here... dies.'

'I DIE?!' Clearly, the Reverend Burton was a comedian, so I chuckled carelessly. 'I don't think so!'

'You lack a sense of dramatic irony, Doctor!' rasped Burton accusingly. My eyes nearly popped out of their sockets as he lifted his cassock and unsheathed an enormous knife. It was twelve inches of Sheffield's finest!

*"Yes, you heard me correctly, Mr Holmes.
That is a Giant Runt."*

'I'll bet that isn't standard issue for a vicar!' said I, hoping to distract him with humour. But in two swift steps he was behind me. He grabbed my hair with one hand and pressed the razor edge onto my windpipe.

'Stay still, Doctor! Professor Moriarty's rules, not mine.'

Petrified, I flicked my eyes over to the fancy pigeon-fancier of Baker Street. I am delighted to report that he looked concerned, his face dark and brooding, bordering on angry. That was only for a few seconds, though, before he laughed a little, shrugged his shoulders and pointed to a cage situated above our heads. Inside, two sleek and elegant black-feathered birds strutted about, cooing their hearts out.

'There is my bird, Reverend. Without a feather of doubt, that is James Moriarty's carrier.'

Scarily, Burton's body went taut! He tightened his grip on my head and his hand tensed on the knife! It seemed as if he had practised his throat-slitting recently but I never had a chance to find out before the light faded away into unconsciousness and my world turned black.

* * *

We arrived back in Baker Street at about six o'clock. The fact that I was walking up the staircase towards our apartment with my head still attached to my neck was living proof that Sherlock Holmes's selection was correct. He was a chap who got me into a hell of a lot of trouble but, luckily, he was incorrigibly knowledgeable.

'It was a good job you know a Hungarian Dark-Legged Highflyer when you see one, Holmes, or I would be a dead man.'

'Oh do stop fussing, Watson! We had to play the game. Remember what Nanny Moriarty told us?'

'That you wouldn't eat your rusks unless the milk was warm?'

Holmes sighed. 'Yes, that too, but, more importantly, and certainly more pertinently, that James Moriarty's father was from Budapest, so the only Hungarian pigeon in the coop had to be the correct choice.'

'Remarkable, Holmes, and thank goodness!' says I, pressing my fingers against the flesh of my throat, still detecting the dried blood from the indentation of the knife.

'Thank goodness you played along Watson,' remarked Holmes, modestly, whilst taking a glance at my neck. 'James Moriarty seeks to humiliate me at any opportunity and instructs his agents to satisfy his sadistic whims.'

'And I just *have* to play along...' muttered I as we entered the apartment. Whilst Holmes rumbled on about Nanny Moriarty, we hung up our coats and hats in the vestibule. I opened the door into the drawing room. There, on the Khaya mahogany dining table, a quite epicurean cold supper was being laid by a confectioner man and his youth assistant.

'What ho, Holmes! What is going on here?'

'Well, Doctor Watson, a supper party without the good manners of telling me first!' exclaimed Mrs. Hudson, fuming mad. She marched over to the great detective and cornered him. 'These men arrived on my doorstep unannounced and demanded they be let in. Oh yes, why not open the door to some complete strangers so they can strip the place bare...'

Mrs. Hudson's devouring of Mr. Sherlock Holmes made me peckish. I went over to the table and admired the spread. Amongst the many inviting dishes of English fare, there was a couple of braces of cold woodcock, a pheasant and a *paté-de-foie-gras* pie, and, now, one less scotch egg. Mmmm! Not bad. There were also several ancient and cobwebby bottles. I poured myself a glass of Pomerol to wash down the breaded sausage; the Chateau Pavie, which was a '65, had a really excellent nose and luscious finish. Suddenly a searing pain shot through the side of my head! Mrs. Hudson had turned away from Holmes and now she was determined to stop me pilfering by actions rather than words, the only ones uttered to me about the rent being overdue. She walked away. Holmes had recovered adequately to dismiss her with a wave of his hand and a curled lip, but, I noticed, he was only brave enough to do so once her back had been turned.

Having laid out all these luxuries the two visitors seemed to vanish away, like the genii of the Arabian Nights, with no explanation or farewell gestures.

'Do they not require payment for their goods and services, Holmes? Not that we have anything to pay them with, of course.'

'Mister Trump is picking up the bill for this, Watson. It is his party. We are merely the hosts.'

At about seven o'clock Lord St. Simon arrived. We heard his step upon the stairs. He came marching in, pointing his cane in front of him again with every other step and dangling his glasses more vigorously than ever, and with a very perturbed look upon his aristocratic features.

'My messenger reached you, then?' asked Holmes.

'Yes, and I must confess that the contents startled me beyond measure. Have you good authority for what you say?'

'The best possible.'

Lord St. Simon sank into a chair and passed his hand over his forehead.

'What will the Duke say? He murmured, 'when he hears that one of the family has been subjected to such a humiliation.'

'It is the purest accident. I cannot allow that there is any humiliation.'

'Ah, you look on these things from a different standpoint.'

'I fail to see that anyone is to blame who stands in this room. I can hardly see how the lady could have acted otherwise, though her abrupt method of doing it was undoubtedly to be regretted. Having no mother, she had no one to advise her at such a crisis.'

'It was a slight, sir, a public slight,' said Lord St. Simon, tapping his fingers upon the table.

'You must make allowance for this poor girl, placed in so unprecedented a position.'

'I will make no allowance. I am angry indeed, and I have been shamefully used.'

'I think I heard a ring,' said Holmes. 'Yes, there are steps on the landing. If I cannot persuade you to take a lenient view of the matter, Lord St. Simon, I have brought an advocate here who may be more successful.'

He opened the door and ushered in a lady and gentleman. I recognised her instantly as the tomboy. It was uncanny, but she really did bear a masculine visage; a square face topped with black wavy hair and brows and a side parting, set against a strong chin carrying a wide mouth whose top lip deserved a moustache (so I placed an imaginary one there). Her saucer-like eyes gave her a feminine cheeriness, so don't judge my observation to be too unkind, but she looked like a mannequin.

'Lord St. Simon,' said Holmes, 'allow me to introduce you to Mr. and Mrs. Francis Hay Moulton. The lady, I think, you have already met.'

At the sight of these newcomers our client had sprung from his seat! He composed himself, stood very erect, chin up with his eyes cast down and his hand thrust into the breast of his frock-coat. He was a picture of offended dignity. The lady had taken a quick step forward and held out her hand to him, but he still refused to raise his eyes. It was as well for his resolution, perhaps, for her pleading face was one which was hard to resist.

'Robert, you look so angry,' said she, in a soothing voice with an accent that can only be described as a rolling twang. 'Well, I guess you have every cause to be.'

'Pray, make no apology to me!' said Lord St. Simon bitterly.

'Oh, yes, I know that I treated you real bad, and, that I should have spoken to you before I went, but I was kinda rattled, and from the time when I saw Frank here again, I just didn't know what I was doing or saying. I only wonder that I didn't fall down and do a faint right before the altar.'

'Perhaps, Mrs. Moulton,' said Holmes, 'you would like my companion and me to leave the room while you explain the matter?'

'If I may give an opinion,' remarked the strange gentleman in a clipped colonial, 'we have had just an itsy-bitsy too much hush-hush tucked away over this business already. For my part, I would like everyone to hear all about it. Why don't we tell you all the story?'

He was a small, wiry, sunburned man, with a sharp face, rather like a racing ferret. He bore an alert manner that was open and honest.

'Pray, continue,' said Holmes, relaxing back to composure.

'Then I'll tell our story right away,' said the lady. "Frank here and I met in '81, in Mc.Quire's camp, near the Rockies, where Pa was working a claim. We were engaged to each other, Frank and I; but then one day father struck a rich pocket, and made a pile, while poor Frank here had a claim that petered out and came to nothing. The richer Pa grew, the poorer was Frank; so at last Pa wouldn't hear of our engagement lasting any longer, and he took me away to 'Frisco. Frank wouldn't throw up his hand, though, so he followed me there, and he saw me without Pa knowing anything about it. It would only have made him mad to know, so we just fixed it all up for ourselves. Frank said that he would go and make a pile, too, and never came back to claim me until he had so much as Pa. So then I promised to wait for him to the end of time and pledged myself not to marry anyone else whilst he lived.'

'Then I said why shouldn't we be married right away, then?' continued Mr. Moulton, 'and then I will feel sure of you; and I won't claim to be your husband until I come back.'

''Yes, well, Frank and me, we talked it over,' interrupted the tomboy, 'and he had gotten fixed up so nicely, with a clergyman all ready and waiting, that we just did it right there; and then Frank went off to seek his fortune.

'The next I heard of Frank was that he was in Montana, and then he went prospecting into Arizona, and then I heard of him from New Mexico. After that came a long newspaper story about how a miner's camp had been attacked by Apache Indians, and there was my Frank's name among the killed. I fainted dead away, and I was very sick for months after. Pa thought I had a decline and took me to half the doctors in 'Frisco. Not a word of news came for a year or more, so that I never doubted Frank was really dead. Then Lord St. Simon came to 'Frisco, and we came to London, and a marriage was arranged, and Pa was very pleased, but I felt all the time that no man on Earth would ever take the place of in my heart that had been given to my poor Frank.'

Mr. Moulton clasped the tomboy's hand and gazed lovingly into her eyes, just like a Jersey cow in labour. Then they kissed. Yeuch! These colonials really didn't know how to behave in public! Lord St. Simon looked distinctly uncomfortable and sniffed disapproval. Holmes and I looked away, down at the floor, taking in the detail of the Azerbaijani prayer mat. Then, fortunately, we were saved by a knock on the door.

'Come!' shouted Holmes.

Mr. Aloysius Trump swaggered into the apartment, legs bowed again, as if he was saddle-sore. He took in his surroundings, his eyes alighting on the people that he recognised and moving on until he noticed Frank Moulton in a clinch with his daughter. Suddenly his face reddened.

'You! It is you who have taken advantage of my little gal!?' shouted he, his arms waving up and down.

Before the racing ferret could introduce himself, Hatty Moulton prised herself away from him. "Pa-pa!" she cried, and threw herself at her father, wrapping her arms around his neck and blubbing. Mr. Trump tried his best to be angry but her tears soon melted his heart. He soothed her crying by stroking her hair and whispering her name over and over. Holmes and I exchanged glances and then looked over to Lord St. Simon, who remained as stoic as a statue. Once everybody had been introduced and settled down, Hatty continued her story.

'Be assured, gentlemen, if I had married Lord St. Simon first, I would have done my duty by him. I went to the altar with the intention that I would make just as good a wife as it was in me to be. But you may imagine how I felt when, just as I came to the altar rails, I glanced back and saw Frank standing looking at me out of the first pew. I thought it was his ghost at first; but, when I looked again, there he was still, with a kind of question in his eyes, as if to ask me whether I were glad or sorry to see him. I wonder I didn't drop. I know that everything was turning around, and the words of the clergyman were just like the buzz of a bee in my ear. I didn't know what to do. Should I stop the service and make a scene in the church? I glanced at him again, and he seemed to know what I was thinking, for he raised his fingers to his lips to tell me to be still. Then I saw him scribble on a piece of paper, and I knew he was writing me a note. As I passed his pew on the way out I dropped my bouquet over to him, and he slipped the note into my hand when he returned me the flowers. It was only a line asking me to join him when he had made the sign to me do so. Of course I never doubted for a moment that my first duty was to him, and I determined to do just whatever he might direct.'

'And, whilst I apologise for interrupting your story, Mrs. Moulton, I wonder if you may describe to us the gentleman who was standing to the side of your husband?'

'He was an imposing figure of a man, Mister Holmes. About six two. Handsome face.'

Holmes curled his lip, a sign that his deepest deduction in this affair had been confirmed.

'Distinctive facial hair, those 'taches drooping down like that.'

'Green eyes?'

'Yeah! Shining bright. Like emeralds, but with an eerie confidence.'

'Thank you, Mrs. Moulton. Pray, continue with your narrative.'

'When I got back from the church I told my maid, who had known Frank in California, and had always been his friend. I ordered her to say nothing, but to get a few things packed and my ulster ready. I know I ought to have spoken to Lord St. Simon but it was dreadful hard before his mother and all those great people. I just made up my mind to run away and explain afterwards. I hadn't been at the table ten minutes before I then began walking into the Park. I slipped out, put on my things, and followed him. Some woman came talking something or other about Lord St. Simon to me — seemed to me from the little I heard as if he had a little

-57-

secret of his own before marriage also – but I managed to get away from her, and soon overtook Frank. We got into a cab in Gordon Square, and that was my true wedding after all those years of waiting. Frank had been a prisoner among the Apaches, had escaped, came to 'Frisco, found that I had given him up for dead and had gone to England, followed me here, and had come upon me at last the very morning of my second wedding.'

'My ship docked in Southampton harbour,' interrupted Mr. Moulton, 'I was met by a gentleman who said he was a friend of yours, sir'. He nodded his head at Mr. Trump. 'He knew my name and where I had come from. He offered me a ride into town and put me up at Claridges. Well, how could I know that all of this was hogwash?'

'I know all about it. Every detail.' remarked Holmes quietly. 'But let us hear the end of the emotional tale that your good wife is relating to us so patiently.'

Mr. Moulton bowed to his wife. She smiled at him with that manly face, but lovingly. But this is where Mr. Trump interrupted proceedings.

'I'll finish off this emotional tale for you!' said he, angrily, like a bull in a bullring. 'I got a visit by that so-called gentleman, the guy with the green eyes and 'taches. He demanded from me the sum of fifty thousand guineas. Fifty thousand! Over two hundred thousand dollars!'

'Otherwise he would reveal the first marriage of your daughter, Hatty,?' remarked Holmes.

'Why, yes, Mister Holmes!'

'And he would prove his point by producing said husband, who he had locked up in the gilded cage of Claridges, and the marriage into this most noble family, which you so dearly desired, would be no more. Am I not correct, Mister Trump?'

'Not bad, for an amateur!'

'And I take it by your reaction that this blackmail was never offered to you as a solution to the missing bride by Inspector Lestrade.'

'Er, no, he did not!'

'The professionals from Scotland Yard failed you,' said I, putting the boot in.

Trump just nodded, hanging his head in shame.

'So, you refused to pay this gentleman?'

'You bet your sweet Fanny Adams I did! I flipped him the bird!' And this likeable, but irascible, American fellow suddenly threw up his right arm aggressively with a clenched fist and only his middle finger erect. We were all taken aback by this gesture of vulgarity.

'Please, Pa-pa, no!'

Mr. Trump deflated. 'I'm sorry, I forgot where I was... It's a bad habit I picked up from prospecting... But nobody takes down Aloysius Trump, sir! Nobody!'

Mrs. Moulton turned to Lord St. Simon. 'Now, Robert, you have heard all, and I am very sorry if I have given you pain. Frank was all for openness, but I was so ashamed of it all that I felt as if I would like to vanish away. I could not revisit all those lords and ladies sitting around the breakfast table, waiting for me to come back. Frank took my wedding clothes and things and made a bundle of them so that I should not be traced and dropped them away somewhere where no one should find them. It is likely that we should have gone onto Paris tomorrow. How Mister Holmes

What would the Americans do without their fingers?

found us is more than I can think, but his telegram showed us very clearly and kindly that I was wrong and that Frank was right, and that we should put ourselves in the wrong if we were so secret. Then he offered us a chance of talking to you alone, Robert, if we came around to his rooms at once.'

Lord St. Simon had by no means relaxed his rigid attitude but had listened with a frowning brow and a compressed lip to this long narrative.

'Excuse me,' he said, 'but it is not my custom to discuss my most intimate personal affairs in this public manner.'

'Then, you won't forgive me? You won't shake hands before I go?'

'Oh, certainly, if it would give you any pleasure.' He put out his hand and coldly grasped that which she extended to him.

'I had hoped,' suggested Holmes, 'that you would have joined us in a friendly supper.'

'I think that you ask a little too much,' responded his lordship. 'I may be forced to acquiesce in these recent developments, but I can hardly be expected to make merry over them. I think that, with your permission, I will now wish you all a very good night.' He included us all in a sweeping bow and walked out of the room.

I looked across at Sherlock Holmes and sidled up to him, whispering in his ear. 'He hasn't paid. I shall go after him.'

Holmes put a restraining hand upon my shoulder and gave me a look of reassurance that finished off with him closing his eyes. I relaxed.

'I trust you will at least honour me with your company,' said Sherlock Holmes to the Americans. 'It is always a joy to meet an American, for I am one of those who believe that the folly of a monarch and the blundering of a Minister in far-flung years will not prevent our children one day from being citizens of the same worldwide country under a flag which shall be a quartering of the Union Jack with the Star and Stripes.'

I stared at him. It didn't take a grammar school *alumnus* to recognise complete and utter bollocks when he heard it! Regardless, our guests fell about laughing and clapping themselves silly until they sat down at the mahogany for our de-luxe picnic supper.

* * *

When our visitors had left, we sat comfortably in the comfiest chairs by the fire with fine cognac in hand, cigars lit, one Englishman talking to another at the height of Empire, our bond of friendship cemented by sleuthing. There was no man in the world who could fill a third chair, and nor would there ever be.

'The case has been an interesting one,' remarked Holmes, 'because it serves to show very clearly how simple the explanation may be of an affair which at first sight seems to be almost inexplicable. Nothing could be more natural than the sequence of events as narrated by this lady, and nothing stranger than the result when viewed, for instance, by Mister Lestrade of Scotland Yard.'

'Well, yes, Holmes, I see what you mean,' said I, all bluff-and-army-like, 'but we know that Lestrade is an idiot.'

'Yes, Watson, but a useful idiot. When he is engaged upon a mystery such as this, he covers much of the groundwork using his resources and then pitches the results to me. The fact that his deductions are incorrect allows us more time to enjoy life. However, left to his own devices, the Lord St. Simon and Mister Trump would be none the wiser about whether the tomboy was alive or dead.'

'You were not yourself at fault, then?'

'From the first, two facts were obvious to me, the one that the lady had been quite willing to undergo the wedding ceremony, the other that she had repented of it within a few minutes of returning home. Obviously something had occurred during the morning, then, to cause her to change her mind. What could that something be? She could not have spoken to anyone when she was out, for she had been in the company of the bridegroom. Had she seen someone, then? If she had, it must be someone from America, because she had spent so short a time in this country that she could hardly have allowed anyone to acquire so deep an influence over her that the mere sight of him would induce her to change her plans so completely. You see we have already arrived, by a process of exclusion, at the idea that she might have seen an American. Then who could this American be, and why should he possess so much influence over her? It might be a lover; it might be a husband. Her young womanhood had, I knew, been spent in rough scenes, and under strange conditions. So far had I got before I ever heard Lord St. Simon's narrative. When he told us of a man in a pew, of the change in the bride's manner, of so transparent a device of obtaining a note as the dropping of a bouquet, of her resort to her confidential maid, and of her very significant allusion to claim-jumping, which in miner's parlance means taking possession of that which another person has a prior claim to, the whole situation became absolutely clear. She had gone off with a man, and the man was either a lover or was a previous husband, the chances being in favour of the latter.'

'And how in the world did you find them, Holmes, for that was the very finest detective work.'

Sherlock Holmes rose from his seat, with a "Ha!" and a spring in his step as he tugged the bell pull. Then, he stood up straight, looked me in the eye, and revealed his master-stroke:

'Do you remember the third man, Watson? The man who has popped up throughout this sorry story? The man who has not been named, but I knew from the outset who he must be and how he had played his hand in this affair.'

There was a knock at the door, the style of which I knew to be that of Mrs. Hudson's cursory "I-am-coming-in-anyway" style of greeting. Professor Moriarty made his entrance. My goodness he was an imposing figure, what with his six foot two and thicker set frame and flesh than either Sherlock Holmes or I. He was grand, but he was also elegant, almost regal in the way that he carried himself. He disrobed by the vestibule, discharging his cape, gloves, top hat and cane to Mrs. Hudson in a well-rehearsed routine. He stopped and looked at us – he surveyed us – waiting for Mrs. Hudson to leave the room. But she took her time positioning his discarded accessories.

'Come in, James,' said Holmes, in a smooth, purring voice. But Moriarty stood his ground.

'Whilst downstairs, gentlemen, I had provoked myself to advance my temptations to a maximum by joining your little party up here, but it was Mrs. Hudson who abolished my ambitious spirit in an instant.'

'She has a way with words. She is persuasive.'

'Sherlock, my dear fellow,' said he, dropping his voice whilst stealing a glance over his shoulder. 'She is persuasive by use of a side-arm!'

Mrs. Hudson gave me a wink as she left the room.

'Ha! Please, take this seat opposite me by the fireplace...'

The chair I was contentedly encased in, and now being forced to give up, as we shuffled around to mumblings of "move along there, Watson!" and "make way" and "yes, be a good chap and get out the ruddy way" was taken by Professor Moriarty and I was relegated to the raspberry damask Savonarola. Sherlock Holmes descended into his seat.

'The good doctor here asked how I came to find Mr. and Mrs. Moulton. Well, Watson, it was easy enough once I knew that Francis Moulton had been put up at Claridges by the Professor here.'

'But what about the receipt in the pocket, the one for the bed and the sherry?'

'That is the more inexpensive hotel that Francis and Hatty Moulton were shovelled off to once your blackmail had failed. You had to cut your losses, eh Teddy?'

'DON'T CALL ME TEDDY!' shouted Moriarty, leaning forward in his seat and pointing his index finger at the great detective.

Sherlock Holmes smiled to himself.

'That hotel was in Northumberland Avenue. I had a friendly word with the concierge at Claridges and he pointed me in the right direction, so thither I travelled, and being fortunate enough to find the loving couple, I ventured to give them some paternal advice, and to point out to them that it would be better in every way that they should make their position a little clearer, both to the general public and to Lord St. Simon. Then, I was able to invite them over for supper this evening. Thus, the affair was brought to a satisfactory conclusion: Mister Francis Moulton has recovered his wife; Miss Hatty Trump has been reunited with the love of her life and is wedded within her social class; Mister Trump has been extricated from a very expensive marriage contract; and, finally, Teddy here has failed in his blackmail. Ha!'

The Professor bristled at the repetition of his nickname.

'You are such a clever-dick, Sherlock!' said he, almost spitting the words out. But then his mood swerved severely, as indicated by his body language. He sat back in his chair and weighed up the situation, working his mouth as if chewing something, his eyes sparkling humorously, his moustaches bobbing up and down, and his upturned hands wavering, as if to mimic the scales of judgment.

'On second thoughts, I suppose you may have been rather incisive in this instance.'

'Regardless of your lifelong feud,' said I, waving my fingers at them both, 'the real loser in this is Lord St. Simon. His conduct was certainly not very gracious.'

Ah, Watson...' said Holmes, smiling. 'Perhaps you would not be too gracious either, if, after all the trouble of wooing and wedding you found yourself deprived in an instant of a wife and fortune, and all thanks to a man that he was never been introduced to and was acting only in his self-interests.'

Professor Moriarty jumped up. 'I shall suffer these insults no longer. You may think that I failed, but, in fact, and in reality, I succeeded. I may have earned no profit from the blackmail – that bow-legged creature, Trump, is a downy bird – but every man of influence knows now in London *and* on the continent that my threats ring true. I may have lost this battle, Sherlock, but I shall win the war.'

Holmes gave me a familiarly disdainful look of mock anxiety as Moriarty marched over to the vestibule and fumbled with his dramatic accessories. Just before he opened the door, he turned to face us, ready for one passing shot, but Holmes cut him off.

'James, I believe it was a wise man of war who once said: "If you know the enemy and know yourself, you need not fear the result of a hundred battles. If you know yourself but not the enemy, for every victory gained you will also suffer a defeat. If you know neither the enemy nor yourself, you will succumb in every battle."'

'If you insist on quoting me *The Art of War*, Sherlock, bear in mind that he also said that "to know your enemy, you must become your enemy" and this is why I shall prevail over you.'

And with that Professor Moriarty tipped his tile to us and departed.